The Three Little Pigs

Retold by Nicola Baxter

Illustrated by Andy Everitt-Stewart

ARMADILLO

Once there were three little pigs.

"We are going off to see the world," they said.

Goodbye, Mum!

Off we go!

"Be good!" said their mum.
"Look out for the big, bad wolf!"

"We will!" said the three little pigs.

The three little pigs
went down the road.

They met a man
with some straw.

"I will make a house of straw!"
said the first little pig.

And so he did.

The two little pigs went on
down the road.

They met a man with some sticks.

"I will make a house of sticks!"
said the second little pig.

What a good house!

And so he did.

One little pig went on down the road.

He met a man with some bricks.

"I will make a house of bricks!" said the third little pig.

What a good house!

And so he did.

But the big, bad wolf
saw the house of straw.

"Open the door!" said the wolf.

"No, no!" said the first little pig.
"By the hair on my chinny chin chin,
I will not let you in!"

But the big, bad wolf went after him.
He saw the house of sticks.

"Open the door!" said the wolf.

"No, no!" said the second little pig.
"By the hair on my chinny chin chin,
I will not let you in!"

The wolf was cross.

He huffed and he puffed
and he blew the house down!

The two little pigs ran off
to their brother's house.

Oh no!

The big, bad wolf went after them.

"Open the door!" said the wolf.

"No, no!" said the third little pig.
"By the hair on my chinny chin chin,
I will not let you in!"

The wolf was cross.

He huffed and he puffed.
He puffed and he huffed.
But he could not get in.

The wolf climbed up on the roof.

"He is going to climb down
the chimney!" said the first little pig.

So the three little pigs put
a big pot of water on the fire.

He is going up!